Welcome to
Why the
Stomach
Growls

Written by Pamela Duncan Edwards and Illustrated by Bridget Starr Taylor

Author's Note

From ancient times, people have pondered how the first human came to be. Creation myths are stories that have been passed down from generation to generation as each culture tried to answer this mystery. I read many myths before I wrote my story. Although they were different depending on what part of the world they came from, they were also similar in lots of ways. In most of them a higher being, a Great God—or sometimes more than one god—controls the heavens and decides to create a man to live on earth. In a myth from West Africa, the Creator at first makes individual parts until it becomes obvious that this doesn't work. Because it isn't smart in the way it deals with the Creator, the stomach ends up being put in the front part of the body where it is exposed to most of the dangers.

As I wrote, however, the stomach began to take over my story and I began to like it. Although it is naughty, it is also very funny, and I decided it deserved better. I then thought what fun it would be if children were to turn the tale into a play. And that's what happened! This creation myth became my story of a class of imaginative children and their teacher presenting their play just for you. Here it is and I hope you enjoy it!

Pamela Duncan Edwards

To dear Lynda (Baroness Chalker of Wallasey),
to whom Africa really Matters.

With love, Pam

For Melissa Turk and
The Artist Network,

With thanks from Bridget

Sleeping Bear Press™

310 North Main Street, Suite 300
Chelsea, MI 48118
www.sleepingbearpress.com

THOMSON
★
GALE

© 2006 Thomson Gale, a part of the Thomson Corporation.

Thomson, Star Logo and Sleeping Bear Press are trademarks
and Gale is a registered trademark used herein under license.

Printed and bound in China.

First Edition

10 9 8 7 6 5 4 3 2 1

Library of Congress Cataloging-in-Publication Data

Edwards, Pamela Duncan.
Why the stomach growls / written by Pamela Duncan Edwards ; illustrated by Bridget Starr Taylor.
p. cm.
Summary: When the eyes, mouth, arms, legs and stomach are created they all want
to be the boss, but with a little help from their Creator they learn to work together.
ISBN 1-58536-298-0
[1. Behavior–Fiction. 2. Cooperativeness–Fiction.] I. Taylor,
Bridget Starr, 1959- , ill. II. Title.
PZ7.E26365Wh 2006
[E]–dc22   2006015311

Long, long ago, when the stars and planets were freshly made, the Creator noticed that the sun shone more brightly, the rain fell more gently, and the wind blew more softly on one of these planets.

"This shall be a special place unlike any other," said the Creator.
"I shall call it Earth."

Onto Earth the Creator put seas and rivers and left land that seemed just the right size.

But the Creator was not satisfied. "Now I shall make a garden and into this garden I shall put many wondrous things." So a garden came to be and it was a place of beauty and peace.

But after more time had passed, the Creator grew dissatisfied once more. "How sad that none but I can appreciate this place."

So the Creator began to fashion shapes. "I shall give each shape its own job," decided the Creator.

Then, out of the Creator's hands appeared

two eyes to admire the beauty of the garden,

two ears to listen to the garden noises,

a nose to smell the garden's scents,

a mouth to speak pleasant things,

Then the Creator breathed life into one last shape. "You shall be called stomach," said the Creator, poking the stomach in its middle to finish it off.

The stomach waited to hear what job it was to be given, but the Creator was tired and said no more. That made the stomach so mad!

"It's not fair," it grumbled to the other shapes. "Why am I the only one that hasn't got a job? You've all got a purpose. I just lie here all day and I'm BORED!"

"There's nothing we can do about it," said the mouth. "Let's face it, you're *not* important. In fact, you're useless!"

And the other shapes laughed and began to call the stomach unkind names.

"I'll show you!" roared the stomach. "I'll make a job for myself. I'm going to work at being a pest!"

So a pest it became. It interrupted and bothered day and night so no shape could do its job properly.

When the eyes tried to gaze at the blue sky, the stomach rolled in dry fallen leaves, and sent up clouds of dust.

When the ears tried to listen to the wind, the stomach made loud, rude noises to drown the wind's song.

The nose bent to smell the flowers but the stomach flopped about, breaking the flower stems.

As for the legs, the stomach pestered them unmercifully. If they set out to walk through the garden, wriggling their feet in delight, the stomach tripped them up and grazed their knees.

That bad stomach caused so much trouble that the shapes began to quarrel among themselves.

The legs kicked the hands and the hands tripped the feet.

The mouth stuck out its tongue at everyone.

The eyes glared at the ears.

The ears wiggled themselves in a very rude way.

The nose turned itself up in disgust.

"STOP!" wailed the brain. "I can't think straight."

With that, all the shapes began to push each other and a terrible argument started.

The stomach sat behind a bush and giggled.

Suddenly a large cloud formed over the garden and a voice thundered, "ENOUGH!"

The shapes stopped fighting and trembled to hear such anger. Except for the stomach, which had grown bold in its bad ways. It just laughed impolitely.

On hearing such bad manners, the knees knocked together so loudly you could hear them from one end of the garden to the other.

"I allowed you to share the beauty of this garden with me,"
cried the Creator. "But you have proved yourselves unworthy!"

"It's all the stomach's fault!" wailed the mouth.
"It wouldn't leave us alone."

"The stomach was indeed bad," agreed the Creator, "but it was unhappy because it had nothing to do. You could have shown pity. You could have shared *your* happiness."

The legs shuffled in embarrassment and the other shapes looked ashamed. But the Creator was gentle and understood that sometimes kindness has to be learned.

"I have a plan," said the Creator. "I think it will help you work together."

Suddenly a great jostling began to take place. From behind the bush, the stomach watched as the shapes became attached to each other from the head right down to the toes.

"I am satisfied," said The Creator. "From now on you are as one."

"Eyes, you will no longer do anything but see. Ears, you will only hear. If you wish to speak, mouth will do this for you. You will be unable to quarrel ever again. Brain, you are the message center. When you receive instructions, it will be your job to help the part to carry out its desire."

All the shapes were pleased. "Now we'll each be able to enjoy everything the others do," said the mouth as the legs began to dance about excitedly.

But suddenly the eyes looked down and sent a message through the brain, which caused the mouth to say,

"There is a hole in our middle!"

The Creator looked at the stomach lying alone on the ground and said, "In you go. That space is for you."

"What?" cried the stomach. "You think I'm going in there with that selfish lot? Not I!"

But even as it spoke, the stomach felt itself being gently lifted and placed in the hole.

"Let me out!"

it yelled. But then it gave a little wriggle as it found that the hole fitted perfectly. "Well, okay then!" it said grudgingly to the Creator, surprised to find its words coming out through the mouth.

"You are now a body," said the Creator to the shapes, "and this body shall be called *human*. From now on you will work together, each benefiting from the other."

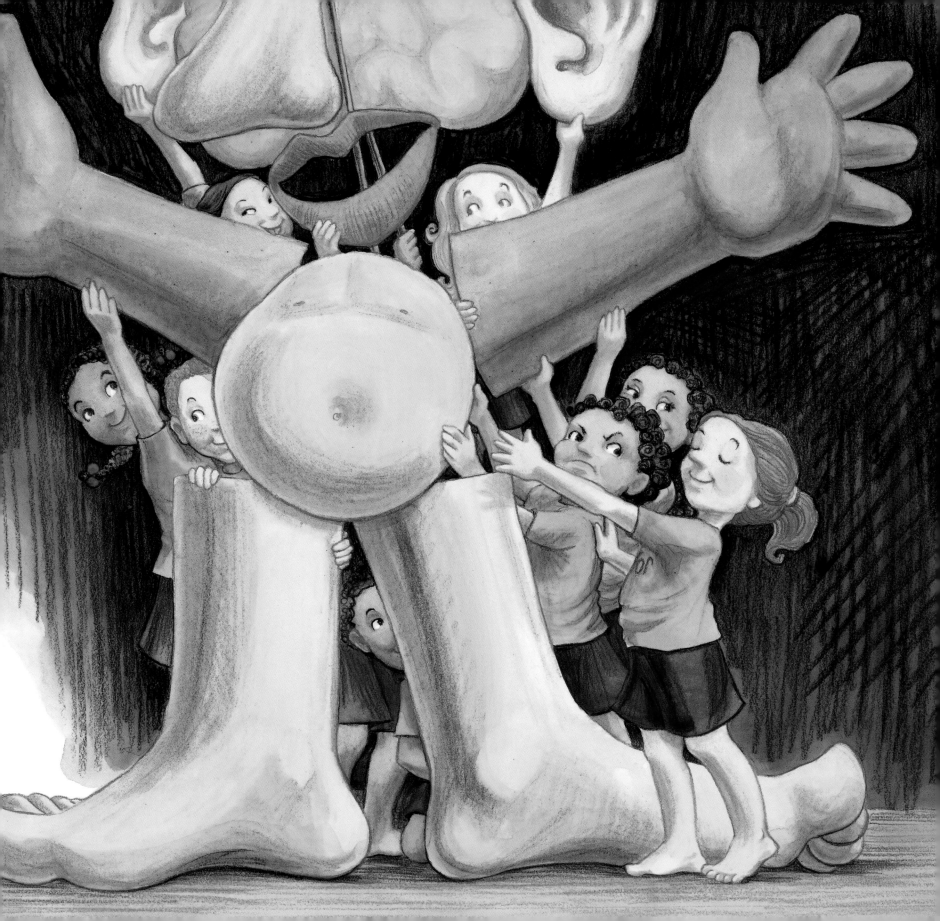

The human jumped up and down on its feet and clapped its hands together.

"But what about me?" wailed the stomach. "I still haven't got a job."

"I have not forgotten you," replied the Creator. "I have decided that this human should now know the joy of food. Because you've had much practice in the art of grumbling, you are given the job of rumbling three times a day—in the morning, at noon, and in the evening. In this way, the human will know it is time to eat."

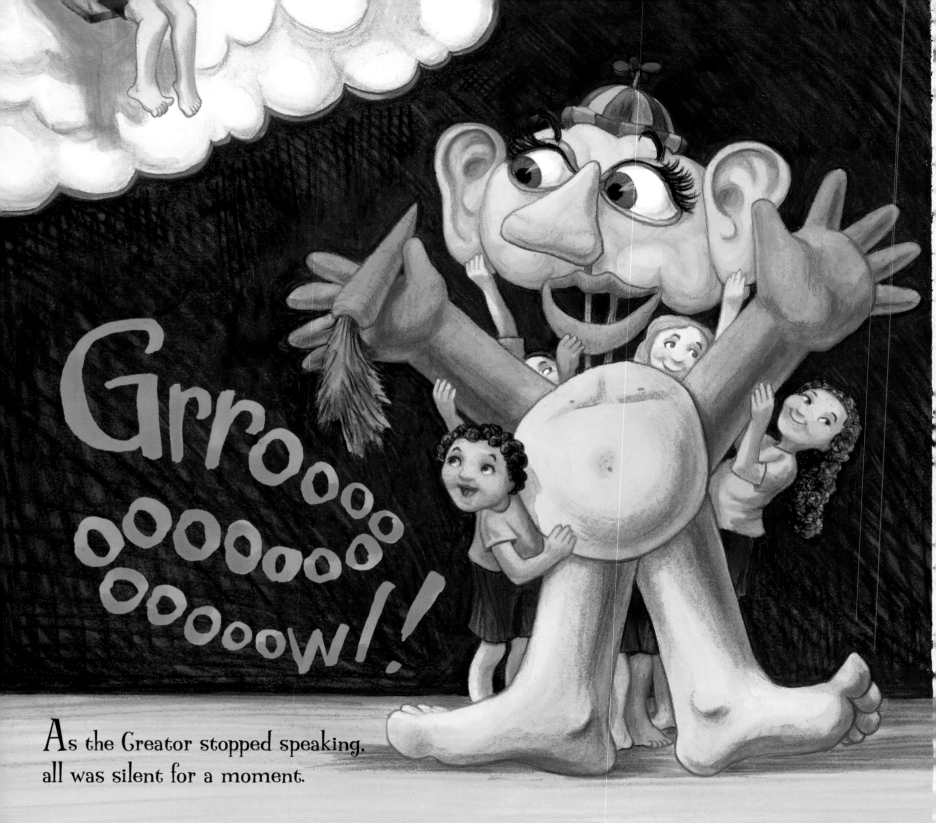

Grrooooooooooooooooow!!

As the Creator stopped speaking,
all was silent for a moment.

Then the mouth smiled and from deep inside the
stomach there came a low **GROWL** of satisfaction.

The End!